INTRIGUE ACROSS
THE KANSAS BORDER

INTRIGUE ACROSS
THE KANSAS BORDER

RAYMOND C. WOOD

INTRIGUE ACROSS THE KANSAS BORDER

iUniverse books may be ordered through booksellers or by contacting:

iUniverse
1663 Liberty Drive
Bloomington, IN 47403
www.iuniverse.com
844-349-9409

ISBN: 978-1-6632-6246-2 (sc)
ISBN: 978-1-6632-6247-9 (e)

Print information available on the last page.

iUniverse rev. date: 04/24/2024

CONTENTS

DEDICATION

Dedicated to my great-grandfather, Edgar Vincent Hazard (1852 – 1915), who gave the idea to write this book, as it's on record that he was living in Kansas as a boy during the Civil War. It's inconceivable to think his father wasn't there to cast his vote for Kansas' statehood to be admitted into the Union as a free state along with thousands of New Englanders who flooded Kansas at this time.

PREFACE

This is a tale about two Irish lads who grew up as the small children of parents who died in early Iowa of the pox. The oldest, Matt, joins the Texas Rangers, while Pat enlists in the Union Army. Later they all come together during a time referred to as "Bloody Kansas" during the Civil War, when Pro-Slavers would vote for Kansas statehood as a slave state, while Anti-Slavers would vote for a free state. In the mix of all this, along with tribes of hostile Indians.

CHAPTER ONE

It was the year 1845 that a covered wagon left Ohio, bound with Rowen and Maureen Davis and their two boys, Matthew and Patrick, for the fertile lands of Iowa, which would reach statehood in the following year of 1846. Despite the many calamities that were part of the frontier, including the Black Hawk War, the parents managed to buy enough land for a crude log house where they, like others in the town called Iowa City, gained a foothold and flourished. The two Davis boys, who were two and four when their parents died of the pox, were luckily taken in by cousins who were living on the outskirts of the town.

By 1860, some homesteaders and others in Iowa wanted to settle nearby Kansas and have it admitted into the Union as a free state, while ruffians from Missouri also had their eye on the land, raiding Kansas in the hopes of securing it as a pro-slave state. It was this struggle that later became known as Bloody Kansas.

CHAPTER TWO

The Davis boys were now 22 and 23. Patrick had joined the Army while Matt went South to Texas to enlist as a Texas Ranger. It was at Fort Des Moines, which would later become Iowa's capital city, where Patrick was quartered. With a little training and sheer will, Matt proved himself and became a Ranger with a pay of $1.25 per day. With an 1860 Army Colt revolver and a Henry rifle, he patrolled Texas, protecting from skirmishes with Comanches and arresting cattle rustlers and wanted bank robbers. He enlisted for a year, and once his time was up, he made his way back to Iowa through Oklahoma, which was mostly Indian territory with scattered white settlements.

In the sparsely settled Tulsa, he went into a saloon, where he saw an older man escorting a young woman to a table, where she looked depressed. At the bar, he asked a fur trapper if he knew anything about them.

"Yeah, I do," said the trapper. "She and her husband, Jerry Dunn, have a cabin about a mile away. He left to the silver lode in Nevada about six months ago. But about a month ago, she got word that he was killed in a camp accident. They have two young girls around two and four.

The man is a cousin who's helping her along with taking care of a wife of his own."

"Damn, mister, you know all about them."

"Well, yeah, so does the whole town."

"That's tragic," Matt pined.

"Yeah," the trapper said. "I've seen it all. There's a young family trying to stake a homestead, but between accidents, bandits, Indian raids, and the pox... Well, it seems to happen all the time."

"Where's the kids?"

"Don't know, reckon with the wife."

"What's her name?" Matt asked.

"They call her Kitty."

CHAPTER THREE

Matt left and headed to the stable to put his horse up then found a place in the barn where he could stay, as the rudimentary layout of the town was not yet equipped with a lodging place for visitors.

In the morning, Matt went to the only eatery in the town, called "The Happy Hen". He had just finished his breakfast when the dark-haired woman called Kitty walked in with, he could only assume, her two children. She was very attractive, but Matt knew she was likely devastated about her husband.

He walked over, saying, "Morning, ma'am. Sorry about your loss."

She looked up, surprised. "How do you know that?"

"A fur trapper told me."

"Oh," she said, lowering her head. "Thank you for your kind words."

As he started to leave, she turned to him. "Wait," she said. "You live around here?"

"No, ma'am, I'm heading for Iowa City."

She looked over to her daughters. "These are my girls. They're two and four. Barbara and Judy."

Matt smiled, "I see they got their mother's pretty looks."

She blushed just as a man walked over with a heavy gun belt, toting a Walker Colt.

"You got business here, stranger?"

The woman quickly said, "Jake, it's okay. The man was just saying good morning."

"Well, I guess you've said it."

Matt put forth, "Just making conversation."

"Like I said, you have said your good morning."

Matt tipped his hat and left the eatery.

CHAPTER FOUR

The next morning, Matt was preparing to continue his trip when he went into the newly general store. To his surprise, the young woman was there getting flour and a few other things.

"Oh," she looked up, noticing him. "Hello again. Sorry about yesterday. My cousin, Jake, is overly protective with strangers."

"And rightly so," Matt agreed. "Let me tell you a little about me so I'm a little less of a stranger. My name is Matt Davis. I've been riding from Texas, where I spent a year as a Ranger."

Kitty's face dropped. "A Texas Ranger?"

"Was." Matt clarified.

Then, Jake pulled up in a buckboard and walked in, staring daggers at Matt. Before he could say anything, Kitty quickly diffused the situation.

"Jake, meet Matt Davis. He was a Texas Ranger and just recently finished his enlistment."

Suddenly, Jake's demeanor changed. "Really, a Ranger?"

"Yeah, I was heading for Iowa City then later Fort Des Moines"

The cousin's tune changed. "Sorry about being rude, but there are too many saddle tramps in this town. I was only protecting my cousin."

"Rightly so, no worries at all."

"Oh, Matt, I should introduce myself. I'm Kitty Dunn."

Matt tipped his hat again.

Jake questioned, "What's that you're packing?"

"That'd be a Colt Patterson."

"Never saw one," Jake said.

Matt smiled. "That Sam Colt is always coming up with something new."

"Well, Matt, why don't you join us for dinner tonight? My wife, Elsee, is a great cook."

"Well, thanks, but I was heading out in a couple of hours."

Kitty chimed in, "Matt Davis, I insist you join us for dinner."

Matt laughed, "Well if you put it that way, I surely will. Besides, one more day won't hurt."

CHAPTER FIVE

Meanwhile, Patrick had been sent out from Fort Des Moines in search of Kickapoo hostiles and they were chased into Nebraska. Then, while on a foray into their camp, the patrol was ambushed, killing one trooper. The rest managed to fight them off despite the Kickapoos having their own stolen rifles. Patrick was captured. He figured they would probably kill him.

After riding for a few hours, they encountered a band of Northern Cheyenne. The two leaders talked and before long the Cheyenne were giving the Kickapoo some buffalo hides in exchange for the soldier. Then, riding into Colorado, which at the time was part of both Kansas and Nebraska territories, Patrick didn't have a clue where he was when the band rode into an Arapaho camp.

After laying out hides and knives, plus metal cookware like pots and pans, which also had apparently been stolen from settlers, as well as some colorful beads, they again traded for the young trooper. Pat was beside himself over the uncertainty of his fate. Soon, the Cheyenne left, and Pat found himself tied against a tree stump.

After an hour or so, two braves untied him and brought him to a council meeting where chief, Chief Stone Bear, and several lesser chiefs were gathered to discuss the captive. In the midst of all the Indians, he saw what looked like a French fur trapper, judging by the looks of his buckskin pants and shirt, both of which were well-worn and had multiple patches. Stone Bear told the Frenchman, Marcel to tell the trooper why he was brought here. Marcel, who had been living with the tribe for nearly twenty years, of course spoke French but now also knew broken English as well as Arapaho and Cheyenne as a result of trading over the years. Marcel told Patrick he would be assimilated into the tribe to take the place of a slain warrior. Patrick blinked, his heart racing.

CHAPTER SIX

Matt gorged himself on venison, root vegetables, and homemade Rye Whiskey as he dined with Kitty and Jake and their families. He soaked some hardtack in the whiskey to soften it up and enjoyed that as well. Matt was enamored in looking at Kitty, who was dressed in a calico dress with a fringed leather shirt and cowboy boots.

Elsee, Jake's wife, asked Matt, "How was the meal?"

He had only one word. "Fantastic!"

Jake led Matt outside to smoke, offering him a small cigar, saying, "Got these in Kansas City. The missus keeps the moist laying against opened tree bark. Keeps 'em fresh."

Jake's wife and Kitty soon joined them outside after putting the children to bed. Matt thought he saw Kitty steal a few glances at him.

Damn, he thought to himself. *A face like that sure makes it hard to want to leave. She's pretty as a Rose of Sharon.*

Kitty asked, "You got family in Iowa?"

"Just a brother, Patrick. He joined the Army last I knew. I'm going to look him up."

Jake inquired, "Is he at Fort Des Moines?"

"Yeah, that's where he reported to."

Jake rubbed his chin. "A couple of months ago, some cowboys were passing through and said the Kickapoos have been acting up. I would think the Army is hot on their trail."

"Well, Jake, that's part of the job."

Jake motioned to Kitty. "Can you get the newspaper? The Weekly Tribune I got from Missouri last month?"

Then he showed news of the Army detachments, mostly keeping peace between pro-slavers and anti-slavers. Matt read it, taking it all in.

"Things are really heating up, especially since Lincoln got elected."

Kitty put forth, "Here in Oklahoma and Kansas, no one is ever far from danger."

Then, Jake and Elsee tended to the few animals they kept, leaving Kitty and Matt to continue the conversation alone.

The two sat on a swing seat Jake had made, as Matt said, "Your husband, like lots of men, tried to hit a vein to bring relief to his family's woes, and I commend him for it."

"Thank you. He would never turn down an opportunity to hit a strike, but it just wasn't to be."

Kitty sighed, bringing her hand to her forehead. "And to think, he was killed by an overturned rail cart."

Matt shook his head. "Sounds like a freak accident."

"Yes, but he will live on in Barbara and Judy."

Matt added, "It must be rough living on the frontier with two little girls and so little law for protection."

"It is, but by the grace of God the Cherokee around these parts have been friendly.

Then, unexpectedly, he clutched her hand. "Maybe you should go to the fort in Des Moines."

"Maybe at some point, but I'll plan my life under the protection of my cousins."

CHAPTER SEVEN

In the morning, Matt bid farewell to Jake, Elsee, and the children, and he was especially sad to have to say goodbye to Kitty, who, in the short time they had spent together, seemed to grow on him like the taste of sweet wine. However, in all probability, he would never see her again.

This area riding to Iowa was begotten with many dangers, including what he feared the most: someone behind a tree or rock with a rifle in an ambush. By luck, and probably divine intervention, he made it to Fort Des Moines.

After only a few days of acclimating himself to the new area, he discovered that his brother had never returned from a patrol where one trooper was killed while the Calvary and Kickapoo were in a back-and-forth cat and mouse game, knowing they had Private Davis. When Matt encountered the lieutenant heading the squad, he learned even more. His brother had likely been trades for buffalo hides to a tribe that had lost a brave in battle. Hearing this, he offered his services to the Army as a civilian scout.

CHAPTER EIGHT

Later, the Army, with even more reinforcements, went on a search and destroy campaign against the Kickapoos while also using the mission to patrol and protect white settlements. Matt, along with the troopers, searched for renegades but to no avail. The force of eight-five well-armed Calvary headed back to the fort after a week.

When Matt returned, he was hit with disturbing news. Cherokee warriors had attacked the outlying farms around Tulsa, killing several people, including Jake and Elsee. Luckily, Kitty and her daughters were in Tulsa at the time, along with five or six other families as well, all headed for the fort since the area had become too dangerous to stay. Evidently, this had all been predicated by the U.S. government giving the Cherokee rotten meat as part of their allotments. Of course, Matt was relieved that an Army detachment had already been sent to Tulsa to escort them to the safety of the fort.

A couple of days later, the covered wagons made their way into the fort, and Matt could see Kitty and her girls had been taken in by Quakers. As they were disembarking, Matt struggled to find the right words to say to her, but she gave him a big hug like he was at last a little sunshine breaking through the horror that had taken place.

Matt conversed, "You're staying with Quakers?"

"Yes, Matt, they're wonderful people. They're great with kids, but they're so regimented."

Matt blinked. "Meaning what?"

"Rules, rules, and more rules."

"Yeah, sounds like them."

"Matt," she said, "I got a little money saved up. I could pay you to take me to the rail-head in Chicago. From there I could take a spur line to Madison, Wisconsin, where I have two sisters."

"I could do that," Matt responded. "Once the territory settles down, but I don't see any clues that it is getting any better. Already there's a lot of talk of Texas and South Carolina forming what they are calling the 'Confederate States of America' under President Jefferson Davis." Matt paused before adding, "No kin of mine."

Kitty, of course, was given living quarters, as best as the Army could give, with two little ones. The other families who lived around Tulsa were also quartered, so it was pretty crowded. Usually, Matt and Kitty would meet at the mess hall for breakfast, and, for Matt, it was the best time of the day when he joined her there. Not trying to be obvious in taking in the 25-year-old dark haired woman's beauty while they were getting to know each other,

CHAPTER NINE

In the Arapaho camp, Chief Stone Bear had Patrick share Marcel's teepee for the time being, with plans to make him into a warrior. Patrick bedded down in the corner as far away from the Frenchman as possible, as he stunk to high heaven.

*Has he **ever** washed his clothes?* Pat thought to himself.

Marcel told him that the chief was almost ready to call on the four stout older squaws, who would transform him into a brave.

"They are eagerly waiting to start the process. Don't worry, lad. Just stay calm. There's nothing to worry about."

"Stay calm when they want me to be one of them? An Indian?!"

"Look, lad, you will be the third white man to go through this in my twenty years here. The first was a trooper who started out alright but became careless and was killed in a buffalo hunt. The second was a prospector, who was a well-respected warrior, and was killed fighting the Crow near Fort Atkinson around eleven years ago."

Patrick was almost afraid to ask what the squaws would do.

Marcel said, "The first thing they will do is strip you and cut any hair from your body."

Pat was trying hard to understand what Marcel was saying in his broken English.

"Next, they cover your body in some kind of paste made from plants and tree bark and cover you everywhere except your face and head."

"What!" Patrick suddenly felt mortified.

"Don't get up a gander, son. There's no pain, except a little when they remove it. This process has been used, as they tell me, since many, many moons ago, since the whites started killing so many of us to take our lands. This Indian way permanently removes any hair. This rite will see you for two days and one night."

"Also," Marcel continued, getting up to light his pipe, "the squaws will go over your body again with knives to make sure all hair is gone. The last thing is that your eyelashes and chin hair will also be treated with the paste."

Patrick looked frozen in fear, and Marcel knew that was not good, so he got in his face.

"Soldier, hear me good. Don't show fear. The squaws treat fear like the plague, so don't give any sign of fear and you will come out like a warrior should. After the ceremony, they will give you a name and a breech clout and moccasins."

Marcel continued, "Being of light skin, in about a week they will treat your body with sunflower oil and pine needle sap. Then your light blond hair will be rubbed in with bear grease. Being in war with the Crow and Blackfeet, you will at some point wear war paint."

The next day, Patrick knew the squaws were coming to get him!!

CHAPTER TEN

At Fort Des Moines, Kitty saw Matt in the road and walked over to him.

"Hi, Mr. Matt. I was thinking me and the girls would love to invite you over tomorrow night for dinner at my place. Will you join us?"

Matt smiled. "Of course, I would love to come."

"Okay, around five would be good."

Matt wondered if he might be able to steal a kiss in light of this invitation.

CHAPTER ELEVEN

Saturday arrived and Matt put on fresh deerskin pants and shirt. Upon his arrival, he spent a little time by the playpen, made by a resourceful trooper, and entertained the kids for a little bit while their mother worked finishing the meal. Kitty had the hearth fired up and was cooking venison and preparing squirrel soup. Boiled potatoes were in a pot along with some other vegetables from the garden. Somehow, she also managed to make an apple strudel. She offered Matt his choice between cider and whiskey. The girls were given a little cornbread with molasses and milk from the fort's cows. At the table, Matt was enjoying Kitty's cooking, and when he finished, he asked if he could light up a cigar.

"Of course," Kitty obliged, before questioning, "You drank the cider but not the whiskey?"

"Yeah, I know. Sometimes it makes me sleepy, and I didn't want to put a stain on the night."

"Well, alright, but I've been sucking on a flask of some homemade Kentucky Moonshine."

"You have?" Matt was surprised.

"Yes, it was my cousin's. Poor Jake used to buy it off someone in Tulsa."

"That's a shame about Jake and Elsee. But you know who is to blame? The U.S. government."

Kitty was taken aback. "The government?"

"Yes, Kitty. The whites are, little by little, driving the red man farther and farther into barren land, while the settlers get all the best farmland. Then the government gives the Indians allotments in exchange, which, in the Cherokee's case, was some tainted meat. The Lieutenant gave me the scuttlebutt. In fact, it happens all the time through these Indian Wars. I can remember not that long ago reading about the great Shawnee chief, Tecumseh, who actually learned to read and write English, can you believe that? Well, anyway, he said 'Where are the Narraganset, the Mohican, the Pokanoket, and many other once powerful tribes of our people? They have vanished before the avarice and oppression of the white man, as snow before a summer sun.' He wrote that not long before he was killed in battle."

Kitty quipped, "I guess now I have a different view of the Indian Wars. Matt, join me on the couch, I have some hardtack if you'd like it."

Then Kitty expressed her gratitude that her little family was under the protection of the fort. Matt let her carry on as he focused on her breasts, straining against her laced top. To his surprise, she put her hand on his leg, triggering his manhood to rise slightly. He was unsure if she had noticed as she got up to grab the hardtack from the hearth.

"Well," he said, "I guess I'll have some whiskey now to soften it up."

"I figured as much, Ranger," she laughed, handing him the flask.

After fifteen or so minutes of them quietly downing the liquor, Matt giggled.

"Now I know why you're purring, Kitten," he said, putting his arm around her.

"Oh, really, Cowboy? That's why I'm purring?"

Matt put his hands on her breasts, and she smiled, giving him a deep kiss. He followed suit as she grabbed his hand, leading him into her bedroom.

"Jump in bed while I check on the girls."

In the interim, Matt quickly shed his boots and clothes. She walked in, doing likewise, and sliding over to him as she was greeted by his hard cock. She went down on it.

"No, Kitty," he gently pushed her away. "Not yet. It's like a Howitzer ready to fire."

She just then kissed him everywhere as he latched onto her beautiful breasts. Things quickly became fast and furious as both were obviously love-starved and the eruption that would be coming knew no boundaries. Within just a few minutes, both were beyond the pale and let loose in a shower of sparks, both of them collapsing in a thousand smiles.

Later, Kitty say she thought for a minute she was in a room full of scented flowers and flanked by candelabras. Then, she grabbed his cock, saying, "But I have the real candelabra down here."

Then they just rolled around and licked and lapped at each other almost to sleep.

When Kitty finally got up, she said, "Hon, stay here while I check on the girls."

Matt was transfixed on this young woman, thinking she's much more than a sizzling, sexy pioneer lass. She's smart, a good mother, and he was sure she didn't let just any man in her bed.

CHAPTER TWELVE

Back with Patrick, they finally came for him, bring him across to the far side of the camp to a large teepee. Inside, it seemed to Patrick that they were all relishing the moment. The four squaws were quick to remove all his clothes as he grimaced. Then they placed his hands upward to a cross stand made from a lodge pole pine tree. He was told to hold it while the squaws removed any hair. At this point in his young life, he had barely fuzz on his back. The squaws were laughing and giggling pointing to him, as they removed his peach fuzz with small knives. To him, it seemed they were making fun of his penis. Then, while two squaws stood in front of him and the other two behind, he was smeared with the concoction of plants and whatever other ingredients until he was completely covered. Patrick could feel it was warm. When they were finished, they attacked his Army uniform with knives, cutting sections to use. After an hour, he was laid down on a bed of pines.

All the next day he just laid there, with them only giving him sips of water from time to time. On the second day, around noon, they started to peel off the now crusted and dried paste, which was no cakewalk, but Patrick bit his lip, remembering what Marcel had said. After all was said and done, he was released to Marcel. Patrick was now an Indian and they would call him Little Buck. They gave him a breech cloth and moccasins it was so strange to wear next to nothing, but the other braves dressed this way, and he would too.

That night, Marcell told him that in the morning he would be given his own teepee. He also divulged that now if he had to defecate, he was to follow the tribe path, which also led to a mountain stream where they got fresh water. Marcel pointed out that Indians used dry grass or a dried corn cobs among other things to wipe themselves. Patrick suddenly remembered hearing that an aunt went to New York City, and they had an experimental flush toilet!

The next day, Patrick, now Little Buck, was given his teepee, and the chief and couple of braves had accompanied him. The chief, then looking at Little Buck, started to laugh. Little Buck looked at Marcel.

"What's wrong?"

Marcel chuckled as well. "Nothing, just the squaws were laughing at you saying, 'Little Buck with a big dink!'".

After leaving the chief, Marcel told him that in the morning, the warriors would start the process of teaching him about weapons and would take him on a hunt. He knew that his main weapon was the 16-shot Henry rifle, but now they were expecting him to take down game with a bow and arrow.

CHAPTER THIRTEEN

At Kitty's, Matt walked out of her quarters just as the Quakers arrived. They took Barbara and Judy away in a buckboard to the other end of the fort.

Matt asked, "Why are they taking the girls?"

"Today, of course, is Sunday, and the girls are going to hear the singing."

"Why aren't you going?"

"I told them I believe in all devotions to God; however, I agreed to share my little ones for them to learn even though I have my own way of doing it. Oh, they tried to convince me to participate, but I kept to my beliefs."

Matt then commented, "They looked rather shocked seeing me here."

"Well, yeah. But to be honest with you, I could give a flying fuck!"

"Wow, Kitty, I can see you got a little Tom Cat in you."

She walked over to him suddenly, grabbing his genitals. "I don't follow the norms like most women, who date for a year before letting their boyfriends touch them. This isn't back East like puritanical Boston. This is the wild west, where you go after what you want. Like a handsome Ranger I just happen to know…"

"Damn, Kitty, I am impressed with your thoughts," he said, giving her a soft kiss.

"Mr. Matt, you want to go riding with me? My mare is getting antsy."

"Alright, let's do it."

Soon, Matt, who was on his own quarter horse, Timber, accompanied Kitty on her mare, Lacey, as they rode within ten miles of the fort, not daring to go further as a result of the trauma of a hostile looking for a coup. After an hour in the saddle, they settled under a cottonwood tree, as Kitty had brought a picnic box with some light lunch, leftover apple strudel, and some more of the Kentucky moonshine. To Matt, it was an extravaganza in the making.

CHAPTER FOURTEEN

Returning to Patrick, who was now plotting to somehow escape back to Fort Des Moines. On the hunt with four braves, despite having to hunt without his rifle, he had caught on quickly, even despite the fact that they were using hand signals. When he got back and went to his teepee, he saw a small boy quickly leave him food and leave, which boded well for him. He then decided he would find a cool pool of water to refresh himself. Knowing that several trails led to the areas of the mountain runoffs, he found one and headed there. Discarding his breech clout and moccasins, he walked into the cold water. Just as he entered the water, he thought he saw someone behind some of the shrub brush. It appeared to be a young squaw with a crossing pattering of deer across her skirt, which had been dyed white.

CHAPTER FIFTEEN

Again, with the lovebirds as they were going back to the horses to return to the fort, Matt watched as Kitty swatted at an insect.

"Darn bug!" Kitty called out.

"Wait, Kitty, don't move," Matt instructed, as it landed on her bosom.

"Where?"

"Don't move," he said, putting his hand on her before adding, "Wait, now it landed on your butt. I'll try to swat it." He reached down, squeezing her derriere.

She turned around laughing, pushing him to the ground. "Bug my foot!" she shouted, jumping on him and planting a lip lock before rolling around in the grass.

When, finally, they headed back to the fort, all Matt could think was that the cake and ice cream was so close, yet so far!

CHAPTER SIXTEEN

At the Arapaho camp, the newly named Little Buck walked back through the path and went to his teepee to eat the meal brought by the young boy, which consisted of wild turkey with potatoes and crushed berries to drink. Then he headed over to Marcel's. Marcel was smoking a pipe when he got there,

"So, Little Buck, it's been three weeks since your new life as a warrior. Are you getting a hang of the Indian life?"

"I'm trying, but I miss my other life."

"Well, that's expected, but you will get to like it."

"One thing I can say, in my short time I have been here, the tribe is very kind to me."

"Yes," Marcel took a long puff from his pipe. "As a rule, the Arapaho and Cheyenne are close as I've seen any two tribes. They also allied with the Lakota Sioux. The Shoshone, Ute, Pawnee, and Crows are enemies. They are further north, what is Montana and Idaho."

CHAPTER SEVENTEEN

As the year 1860 moved into October at the fort, Matt and Kitty were hearing lots of William Quantrill, a southern guerrilla leader harassing Federal troop movements in Kansas. Also, the pro-slavery Missouri ruffians fighting against anti-slavery forces called Jay Hawkers. So, traveling to Chicago, for Kitty was put aside indefinitely. Then, Matt got the word that the Major Benjamin Tanner, the commanding officer of the fort was putting together a two-hundred-force Calvary displacement to seek out Kickapoo renegades, and he, along with John Reno, another scout and a Pawnee as well.

In the mess hall, Matt told Kitty he was also leaving in a couple of hours. Kitty was aghast that he was leaving so suddenly.

"Yes," Matt said, "me also."

Kitty added, "Honey, I thought more or less the Kickapoo moved to the north."

"Could be, babe, but between us I think the major is looking for trouble to make a name for himself."

"Are you serious?"

He grabbed her hand. "That was my take on it."

"How long?" Kitty was getting a little choked up.

"I'm assuming two or three days."

The troops left as planned and rode deep into Iowa, then Nebraska, where a large force of Kickapoos and Sioux forces attacked in an ambush, killing twenty-three troopers and scout John Reno. However, the Army, thanks to rifles and the fire power of Colt .44 caliber and other guns, finally routed them, killing more. When the smoke cleared, the major and his troops headed back to the fort, minus two more soldiers and Matt Davis, who went after them and never returned.

Back at the fort, of course Kitty was devastated her man didn't return. The Army took a big blow with the twenty-three troopers killed, so they were hesitant to search for the men until they could secure more ammo. Finally, they re-armed and for two weeks there was no sign of the three men. Kitty was trying to pull herself together when a buffalo hunter called Zeke saw Kitty in the PX.

"Excuse me, ma'am. Aren't you attached to Matt Davis?"

"Well, I guess you mean he's my boyfriend?"

"Yes, ma'am. I've known Matt since Texas. He's one hell of a buckaroo, that I know. I just know those red skins didn't do him in. He is too smart to be caught."

Kitty wiped a tear. "That's what I've been thinking too."

"Well, ma'am, I'll be pushing out in the morn to go after buffalo. I'll keep an eye out."

"Aren't you worried about renegades?"

"Not one bit. I've been swapping spit with the red men all my life."

"Swapping spit?"

"Oh, that means trading."

"Well, er, okay, mister--?"

"Zeke," the man said. "I'll keep trying to find out if any Indian knows anything."

CHAPTER EIGHTEEN

Back with Little Buck as he left the teepee with a bladder to fill for water, he was walking down to the water where he saw several squaws already there. One squaw stood out. She appeared to be seventeen or eighteen and exceedingly beautiful. She was there with several other younger squaws. With the chillier weather, Little Buck wore leggings and a buckskin shirt. He went to the edge of the pool and started to fill the buffalo skin bladder. As he did so, the younger squaws were all acting silly, looking at him, as the beautiful teenage squaw was trying to act clueless to their giggling. Little Buck knew the telltale signs for remembering seeing her sewing clothes one day with older squaws and how she was staring at him. Of course, he stared back. Now practically face to face, he saw her put the full bladder of water in a sling over her shoulder as she turned to leave. He walked over and, using the few words he knew, attempted to tell her that he would carry her water, which she accepted. With the giggling small children behind them, they made their way back to the camp. The squaw, who was called Sundew, thanked him quickly and then Little Buck departed, but he knew that she was infatuated with him. As he walked back to his own teepee, he got this unfamiliar warm feeling that seemed to make him smile. In fact, now every time he saw her, even if it was only just a glance, the feeling seemed to be stronger each time.

CHAPTER NINETEEN

Matt Davis had been in a deadly fight with five Kickapoos along with a trooper who caught an arrow through his neck and died instantly. His Henry rifle barrel was red hot, and he knew he had killed two of them. The Kickapoo apparently had had enough and rode away, taking their dead with them. After considerable time, he put the slain trooper across an Indian Paint as his horse was nowhere to be found. Unfortunately, there was no trace of the second trooper.

At the fort, they opened the gate and inside Major Tanner's office, he quickly brought him up to speed on what happened. Then he was told the horrible news that a typhoid epidemic had hit the fort and all civilians were evacuated to the stanch anti-slavery town of Lawrence, Kansas. He was also told that Kitty Dunn and her children left with the Quakers. Initially, he was overwhelmed with relief. Although the Kickapoo threat had been marginalized for the most part, he decided that he would resign as a scout and start seeking out Kitty to join her.

In a few days, after rearming himself with ammo, he set out with a packhorse for Lawrence, which was 234 miles of dangerous terrain, mostly from the Missouri ruffians.

Finally arriving, Kitty was overjoyed when she finally saw him come to the shelter. After reuniting, they went to her apartment in the center of town.

"Not bad," Matt exclaimed.

"Yes," Kitty said. "The Quakers bring us clean water from an underground well, and people all around have brought us fresh food from their gardens. However, the downside is that we only have a chamber pot to relieve ourselves."

Matt looked straight in her eyes. "Kitty, in Texas I bought a couple acres along the Rio Grand River. Hopefully, when things ever calm down, if you would like, I would love to build a cabin there with all the fresh water we need."

"Oh, Matt," she said, hugging him.

Matt asked, "Where's the girls?"

"One guess."

"With the Quakers."

Then she marched him into the bedroom, removing her garments as they went, and laid under the bed covers. Matt unbuckled his gun belt and peeled off his clothes.

"Give me a minute," he said as he got out of his Union shirt and went to where the water was kept so he could soap up and wash his body, getting all of the residuals off from the dusty ride on the frontier.

Kitty watched as he walked over, his hard cock on full display as he got under the covers.

"Oh, Matt, my cowboy! I thought you would never arrive!"

Matt laughed as he took in the wildflower scent of her.

She smiled. "In that tiny bathtub I managed to take a long bath in perfumed waters."

"And" Matt grabbed her, saying, "I love tasting you, girlfriend.

"And I you," she returned, as she went down on his burning manhood.

Before he would burst, he gently pulled her up. "Not yet, Queen Bee. After riding, fighting Indians, and enduring the weather, I just want to feel your bare, soft body for all eternity."

"I'll always be yours, Ranger." Then, again, she went down on it.

This time, there was no stopping her, and Matt's hold-off turned to mush as Kitty brought him to the moon and back. It was only a few minutes before his member was once again like a stone post as Kitty reeled back onto his chest, steering his member into her.

"Ah," Matt exhaled.

On top, Kitty then went up and down, driving both of them crazy for a good number of minutes before they both let loose.

All Kitty said was, "Oh my God, Ranger, are you for real?"

Matt didn't respond, too preoccupied with sucking her nipples. After more feeling each other up and then some, they had to get up, as the Quakers would soon be there with the girls.

Once the girls arrived home, Matt kept them entertained while Kitty cooked up a couple of steaks, courtesy of the Quakers, who always seemed to find ways to please her so they could keep the girls in their indoctrinating way of life. Of course, during these hard times, Kitty sometimes had to bend a little on what she liked about them and what she didn't like.

"Honey," Kitty began. "Where are you going to stay?"

"At the Lawrence Inn."

"I would love for you to stay with me, but you know what the Quakers would do. They would certainly call us ungodly. Living together unmarried, living in sin."

"Of course, Kitty. That's what I wouldn't. I want what's best for you and the little ones. It's the right thing to do."

CHAPTER TWENTY

Later, Matt went to a saloon owned by a German immigrant; it was called The Kansas Moon. There, everyone was talking Civil War as the South was rearming its Army and getting battle-ready for the impending war. Lawrence was full of intrigue, and no one could be trusted. The Kansas Jay Hawkers were the most prevalent in the town, but there were a number of pro-slave families here throughout. In the bar, everyone was sure that, at some point, there was going to be something that would spark and set the entire country into the full blaze of war. Of course, hundreds of people from the North were rushing to Kansas, wanting to swell the anti-slavery vote on statehood. The pro-slavers from Missouri were harassing people coming in, who were of course going to vote for a free state, and in many cases, they were beat up or otherwise intimidated. A good number came from New England states, especially Massachusetts, as Lawrence was founded by abolitionist Amos Lawrence in 1854.

Matt could hear two men arguing on the slavery question. One seemed to be a cattleman by the odor of his clothes. The other man, wearing thick glasses, could see the cattleman getting angrier and angrier and his hand twitching closer to the revolver hanging from his waist. Matt approached them.

"Gentlemen, calm down before things get out of hand."

The cattleman got in Matt's face. "Mind your own business, stranger!"

Matt tipped his hat back. "It's plenty my business when a gun might go off and anybody could get shot, including me."

"That's too fucking bad," the cattleman said, shoving him.

Before the man knew what had hit him, Matt whacked him with a solid left score to the face and another hard belt to the stomach. The big man was laid out. As he grabbed the bar to lift himself, he went to his gun, but the bartender pointed a shotgun to his nose. Matt grabbed the pistol, handing it to the bartender.

The sixty-some off year old bartender yelled in broken English, "Get out now!"

Matt was ready for a couple more whacks when the cattleman knew he had had enough and left.

The smaller, bespectacled man walked over to Matt, saying, "Thanks, Mister. I was unarmed."

"Yeah, I could see that. My advice to you… I would carry. It's awfully dicey in this town."

In an effort to tamp down the volatility of the moment, the bartender, who also happened to be the owner of The Kansas Moon, yelled in his thick German accent, "Drinks on the house!"

CHAPTER TWENTY-ONE

At the Arapaho encampment, as the sun was rising over the Rocky Mountains one crisp October morning, Little Buck lay in his teepee, when suddenly he heard yelling and screaming. Looking out, the Arapaho were fending off an attack by a smaller number of Crows. It was a sneak attack that had been interrupted by an alert guard. In the chaos, the Arapaho countered with volley of arrows along with Chief Stone Bear shooting Little Buck's Henry rifle. One Arapaho was killed, along with two Crows, but they captured the sub chief leading the attack.

After everything calmed down later in the day, Little Buck joined Marcel for some rabbit stew.

Marcel finally addressed the situation. "That was a bad thing that the Crow got close enough for an attack, and Stone Bear is beyond mad it happened. Young Hawk, a young warrior, was killed."

Little Buck asked, "What are they going to do with the Crow?"

Marcel lit his pipe. "Son," he said, "in two days, after they finish getting all the information from the Crow, which they might even have by now, the Crow called Claw Hand will be forced to run a gauntlet three times. Then the older squaws will tie him to a wooden frame to torture him with pointed sticks from the fire until he dies."

Little Buck flinched. Marcel noticed, saying, "Little Buck, it's the way of some tribes of the red men against their enemies."

Marcel then added, "When the time comes, all the tribe will be cheering on the torture of the Crow. You also must be there."

CHAPTER TWENTY-TWO

In the days after, the Crow was surprisingly given food and drink. Then, some kind of ceremony was afforded the doomed brave before he was dragged out to the area beside a roaring fire with eight braves on each side of the gauntlet. They would whack and flay his naked body unmercifully. Little Buck would see almost the whole tribe yelling and cheering as Claw Hand ran the first gauntlet. He made it to the end, covered in blood from the countless blows on his body. The second time, he barely made it, as the braves took revenge out on him. Little Buck knew he would never run the third without falling. He could see Sundew on the other side with all the younger women and children in what was a big spectacle, almost like the crowds at rodeos he had seen.

He was right; the Crow fell down on the third run and the braves dragged his bloody body to the frame, which had been setup like a tripod. Then, in more cruel torture, the squaws stuck their pointed sticks into the fire and then into the already bloodied man. It was something he hoped he would never see again. After at least an hour, the poor Indian's ungodly screams became softer and barely a whisper, having blown out his voice entirely, when two of the squaws gave him the 'coup de grace' by jamming their burning sticks into his anus. Then his body was thrown into the great fire. The Crow, Claw Hand, who had led the attack was not nothing more than smoldering ashes.

After this event, the tribe danced and rejoiced that the perpetrator was no more. They feasted on buffalo and deer meat, along with some kind of juice from wildflowers, which apparently had properties of hallucinations or gave some others the false sense of invincibility.

Later, Little Buck found out that Chief Stone Bear and some others were drinking whiskey they had traded from the whites, and they could barely stand. Little Buck joined Marcel.

Marcel, of course, never went to these kinds of things where the Indians would call their terrible wrath down upon their enemies. Instead, Little Buck found him making a drink from a box-elder tree. He boiled the sap to make sugar and added choke-berries. Actually, Little Buck thought it was pretty tasty.

Later, Little Buck joined the younger braves on a hunt for buffalo, but the Indians realized that the buffalo had been cut down in many places by the white men for sport. They were fewer and fewer with each hunt. This time, Little Buck was given an Appaloosa horse of his own and, for the first time, he hadn't felt the pull of his plot to escape back to the fort, but instead more drawn to the young squaw called Sundew.

One morning at sunrise, Little Buck was ready to get up when he heard his name called out by a young woman. He opened the flap and could see it was Sundew. She slowly told him in her language that she had made some cornmeal for him to eat. He thanked her and, with a smile, she departed.

Darn, he thought, *why did she leave? How can I have more than a few minutes with her?*

CHAPTER TWENTY-THREE

At Lawrence, Kansas, as Matt went to a saloon for a meal, he overheard a couple of people saying that Leavenworth, Kansas had a reputation of a strong town in the rule of law. They said that many families were drawn there, making him think of how much he would love to take Kitty there, but he debated whether she would agree to go, and he knew for sure the Quakers certainly wouldn't.

Kitty had just dropped off the girls with the Quakers by Buck Board as they were having a childcare's event with several kids from a number of families, when he stopped her.

"Hi, Mrs. Dunn, Who's wagon?"

"Charlie Pina, the blacksmith, let me borrow it. So, Matt, what are you up to?"

"Well, at this moment, I'm flirting on your breast."

"Is that a fact, cowboy? Do you do that often?"

"Just when I see you, Mrs. Dunn."

"So, what's the bottom line here?"

"I reckon it's to play out my fantasies."

"Really? Have you done that before?"

"I have, but I'm selfish. I want more."

"Well," Kitty smiled, "I passed a Live Oak tree grove and the grass looked so lush and thick…"

"Really? Do you mind showing me?"

"Tie Timber at the rear and I'll show you."

After riding for about ten miles, they entered a little side trail to the grove and disembarked.

"Come on, Matt, it's shady under the tree."

They both sat down on the moss and grass when Kitty moved toward him, standing up and slipping off her dress.

"No slips?" Matt asked.

"Believe me, babe, I discard it as much as possible."

Matt grinned and grabbed her, planting a lip lock.

Before long, both were in the buff, taking their time with the foreplay, as Matt said, "Honey, what's that between your legs? A freckle?"

Before she could say anything, he was licking it, then went into what he called a tight little golden vault. It was then that Kitty let out a tantalizing sound of bursting ecstasy!

Much later, as they were laying on the soft turf, Matt confessed, "I feel like I'm with the Queen of the Stars when I make love to you, Kitty Cat."

"Yes, cowboy, I feel that it's only a dream, but then I realize it's not dream. It's just my hunky cowboy from down Texas way."

She grabbed his penis, saying, "I really know now what they say is true. Things really are bigger in Texas."

They both laughed before starting again. Matt and Kitty were carrying on their out of wedlock relations and couldn't care less what the Quakers or anybody else thought.

CHAPTER TWENTY-FOUR

Matt got word that Ben Bird, a well-known hunter and trapper, was at Topeka, Kansas the soon to be the capital. Matt knew he had to get a hold of him. The next day, as kitty was caring for her girls, Matt rode over and dismounted. When he went into her apartment, Kitty looked up as she finished feeding the children, and noticed he was wearing chaps and a thick bandana with a full cartridge belt.

Before she could say anything, Matt voiced, "Sweetheart, I'll be gone for a few days at the minimum, or maybe quite a spell."

"And?" she questioned.

"I got word that Ben Bird is in Topeka. He's known for helping settlers from time to time to locate lost loved ones or those that have been captured by tribes. You know, of course, I've been searching for my brother, Patrick."

Kitty walked up to him. "I know what you're going to say next. You're going to hire him to help you find him."

"Yes, Kitty, I've known of him from when I was a Ranger. He helped us in chasing Sam Bass. He has the instincts of a Comanche. I must find out where Patrick is, dead or alive."

Kitty brushed Judy's hair, trying not to let him see the tears that welled up in her eyes, her face spelling out her blatant fear. "You be careful, Matthew Davis."

He hugged her. "I will."

CHAPTER TWENTY-FIVE

As he headed for Topeka, well aware of the dangers of his mission, he knew the talk of the Civil War was getting stronger and the Kansas frontier was rife not only with Indians but with Missouri ruffians and Kansas Jay Hawkers. He knew it was probably a long shot, but he had a feeling his brother was alive. With his trusty horse, Timber, and another packhorse, he left for Topeka. He had wired him earlier, so he knew Bird would be waiting.

That night, he met with Bird, a 55-year-old veteran of the Mexican War with a long shaggy, red beard and matching hair. In the morning they left Topeka and headed for the Cheyenne encampment, with Bird having traded with them the year before, he believed it would be a good place to start. Matt noticed his packhorse was loaded up with all kinds of stuff that the Indians would trade for.

Late in the afternoon, they reached an area close to the village where two braves rode up on their paints. They didn't look too friendly.

"Don't worry none, Matt. They know me."

After being led into the camp, the Cheyenne were apprehensive about Matt, but kept their hatred of the whites at bay, knowing Bird always had cookware and blankets and other things to trade.

After the Pow-Wow, and with Bird speaking their lingo, the Chief said, "This past spring, a band of Northern Cheyenne from Montana traded away a white captive for hides."

Bird then said, "That's the break we have been looking for. I'm pretty sure your brother was the one that they traded for. However, the chief doesn't know who they traded with. It could be with Pawnee, the Lakota Sioux, or maybe the Arapaho."

Matt said, "Any way we can find out more?"

"Well," Bird said, his thinking coming full circle. "The Pawnee and the Lakota are at war. I reckon the Arapaho might have him. They are in Colorado territory. It's been a spell since I've been there. Several miles from Sand Creek. It will take two or three days to ride there. We have to be ready for any Crow. There are a handful around these parts, as well as some Comanche, who took down a five-wagon train heading to Denver last year. Had them a fight for their lives until a Calvary patrol out of Denver drove them off. We'll have to keep cooking fires as small as we can at night."

They bedded down for the night, with Matt taking the first watch after they drank a little of homemade whiskey from Tennessee from Bird's flask along with dried meat and hardtack.

CHAPTER TWENTY-SIX

At the break of dawn, it was already extremely hot for this time of year and they had soldiered on for two days when, in the distance, they saw three Indians on Appaloosas.

Ben quickly said, "Matt, they're friendly. Nez Perce out of Idaho."

Confronting them, Matt was stunned that old Ben could talk their lingo. It was beneficial that it even happened, as Ben traded a couple of knives for several freshly killed rabbits.

After they left, Ben said, "Matt, let's cook up the rabbits while they're still fresh."

Matt was more than willing. Plus, the fire would be less noticeable in the light of day.

Once they finished eating, they rode on into the late afternoon, when Matt spotted three more Indians on horseback. Ben took out his spyglass, looking ahead.

"Three Pawnee. Let's stay out of sight."

CHAPTER TWENTY-SEVEN

Around seven that night, Bird pointed out smoke in the distance.

"Matt, that smoke. I reckon it's the Arapaho camp."

As they rode in, about six painted warriors on horseback confronted them, but Bird spoke to them easily in their Plains Algonquin language, telling them he wanted to trade. One of the warriors recognized Bird and motioned them to follow. As the two white men entered the camp, the squaws and children were astonished by their presence, especially gawking at Ben's red hair and beard. Matt could see most of the braves were in war paint, likely because they were at war with the Crow nation.

Chief Stone Bear confronted them as Bird spread his goods out on the ground. Although Bird seemed to connect with them, Stone Bear called for Marcel to be involved. The Arapaho traded for many pots and pans, cloth and beads, knives and hoes; Bird, in kind, got furs and beaver pelts as well as honey and wild berry juice in dried gourds.

Bird then asked Marcel about Patrick.

Marcel, in his late sixties, said, "The soldier you're referring to is now a warrior called Little Buck, who has been adopted into the tribe. He should be back soon from a hunt."

Matt didn't know what to say or how to act. Stone Bear motioned them to his teepee to smoke a peace pipe.

Inside, Marcel relayed what the chief said, telling them that the Arapaho were not at war with the Blue Coats, but tensions were building as a result of soldiers from Denver having had run-ins with the tribe.

Marcel added, "Your brother has been welcomed into the tribe."

After they all smoked the pipe, Stone Bear got word that Little Buck was back from the hunt and sent for him. As Matt sat quietly around the circle, Little Buck walked in. Matt hardly recognized him, as his face and arms were fully painted, his once yellow hair was dyed black and woven into braids. He was wearing a breech clout with leggings and a buckskin shirt.

He just looked and said, "Brother Matthew."

CHAPTER TWENTY-EIGHT

The wise old chief told Marcel to leave with him and let the brothers be allowed to talk. Matt stood up, not knowing if he should embrace his brother or not. However, Little Buck did.

Matt said, "I didn't know if you were still alive."

"Yes, Matt, very much so. I am part of the tribe now, and I am a changed person. These Arapahos are now family to me."

Matt was taken aback somewhat. "So, brother Patrick, you have come to like being an Indian?"

"Well, at first, I would have to say no. I wanted to escape, but then I discovered that the tribe treats everyone like a big family, including me, as everybody watches each others back. Also, they are generous, like lots of people were in Iowa when we were growing up. Then, I have an affection for a squaw called Sundew."

"Alright," Matt said. "What you're saying is that you're going to live your life as an Arapaho?"

"Yes, Matt, I do now. How goes it with you? You're not a Ranger still, are you?"

"No, enlistment was only a year. Now I am living in Lawrence, Kansas, and I too have an affection for a woman, Kitty Dunn."

Little Buck then said, "On hunts I miss my Henry rifle. The chief's got it now."

Matt smiled. "Brother, before I left, I brought a Colt Army revolver and fifty rounds in case I needed them to help me find you."

"That's good, brother," Little Buck voiced. "We have been in a heated war with the Crow."

Little Buck pointed. "Follow me, brother, to meet Sundew."

Rapping on where she lived with her grandmother, Sundew came out and Matt could see she was exceedingly attracting, wearing a full deerskin skirt. In Arapaho, Little Buck did his best to tell Sundew about his brother.

Sundew smiled, saying, "I am honored to meet you."

Little Buck told him what she said.

"Tell her the same for me," Matt affirmed. "Well, Patrick, or should I probably say Little Buck, it's the first of November now, so Bird and I will be pushing on. We don't want to run into any snowstorms."

"Yes, here in the Rockies the snow gets very bad. Sometime I will return the visit to you in Lawrence."

"That would be good, Little Buck, however, there's riders out there who would shoot you because you're an Indian. Plus, these times are pointing to a Civil War between the states on the slavery question. The frontier is dangerous as all hell."

Little Buck followed up, "I will follow the wisdom of counsel to see when would be best to go."

With that, Matt and Ben spent the night at the Arapaho camp. Then, at the break of dawn, Little Buck and three warriors escorted them around ten miles before bidding them farewell.

CHAPTER TWENTY-NINE

Matt, of course, was grateful that Ben helped him reunite with his brother, but after paying him handsomely his money was now pretty much depleted. He knew he needed to find something to keep the cash coming in, and when they got back to Topeka, he got an opportunity as the new sheriff. Once more, as with his Ranger enlistment, he only agreed to a year.

Wiring Kitty, he told her about his now Indian brother, Little Buck, and that he had found work as a sheriff. Of course, that didn't bode well for her. She knew she wouldn't see him for quite a while, but she knew her man wasn't the type to malinger.

CHAPTER THIRTY

The first couple of months, Matt had only the routine of rowdy cowboys acting up in the saloons or an occasional thief. That was, until his newly appointed deputy, Roy Jackson, walked into the sheriff's office with some big news.

"Matt, around thirty riders rode into that big saloon, The Cactus Hole. Many wearing confederate patches."

Matt put forth, "That's not good. It could only mean trouble."

As it was an extremely frigid February day in 1861, Matt walked out to see a score of men leading their mounts to the nearby stables.

Roy said, "Quantrill has been active in the territory. Do you think they could be part of the gunmen?"

"Could be," Matt supposed. "They have been raiding border towns. Roy, let's load up the two Henry's and the Spencer."

Matt began putting on his two-holstered gun belt, toting two Walker Colts.

A couple of hours went by when they heard shots. The town barber came flying into the office.

"Those riders shot a man on the street!"

Matt instructed Roy to grab the shotgun, and they headed toward the saloon, seeing a cowboy dead in the street. As they walked in, the loudmouth bunch could see the badges of the lawmen.

One of the men, likely the leader, said in a sneer, "Well, boys, the law is here."

Matt, in no uncertain terms, called out, "Who shot the man?"

Various murmured responses were returned, a mix of "What man?" and "Shot who?".

Matt told the leader, "Quit playing or I'll arrest you all!"

The leader, Domingo, said, "What do you think, boys? They want to arrest us all!"

The group laughed along with their leader as Domingo reached for his gun. But Matt was too quick, and his Colt blazed, hitting him in the leg and taking him down. Two cowboys went for their side arms when the shotgun roared, pushing one back to the bar, while Matt killed the other. The gang, seeing what was left of their com-padre hit by the shotgun, his head nearly decapitated, backed up toward the swinging doors, slowly exiting.

One of them yelled, "You got a fight coming!"

Matt said, "You got the wrong town!" as he aimed straight for his head, killing him instantly.

The gang dragged Domingo out and quickly retrieved their horses, clearing out and riding away from the trigger-happy sheriff.

Roy gasped, "Shit, I would never believe it."

Matt put his spin on it, "These kinds of men live by the gun and die by the gun."

Roy wondered aloud, "Do you think they'll be back?"

"It's a good chance they will be…" Matt trailed off before adding, "How many scatter guns does Cogswell have?"

James Cogswell was the owner of the gun shop.

Roy scratched his head. "I think at least four."

"Grab them. Tell Cogswell I'm taking them because of an immanent invasion of the town."

Roy looked perplexed. "Immanent invasion?"

"After that, round up every man in town who owns a rifle and have them report to me."

CHAPTER THIRTY-ONE

March arrived and Little Buck was finding any excuse to be near Sundew. One late afternoon, as Little Buck was bundled up in a buffalo coat, he saw her teepee open and watched as a smiling Sundew motioned for him to join her. He went inside, where her grandmother was stoking the fire in the middle of the teepee. She motioned for him to sit down. Sundew brought him potato stew, which warmed him up considerably. For the first time, Little Buck was finally close to her, and she was well in a mindset of, as the Arapaho would say, a happy trail. The grandmother didn't say anything, only moving to the corner of the teepee so her granddaughter could have a more private conversation with the former soldier turned Arapaho warrior. With few words between them, Sundew and Little Buck did their best to communicate and sat together smiling. Of course, this once again gave him that unfamiliar feeling in his stomach, which only seemed to accelerate as he focused on the young maiden.

After an hour or so, Little Buck headed back to his own teepee with a bladder bag over his shoulder, filled with food and wild berry juice. Returning to his teepee, one thing always stayed with him. He made sure every night his body was clean before he settled in under the bear hide that made up his bed. He had stripped off his buffalo coat along with his deerskin shirt, leggings and high boots. Then, removing his breech clout, he began cleaning himself up with ground corn cobs as he was shown when he first came to the tribe. In a mirror that was traded from the fort, he could he that he was no longer the puny boy he had been as Patrick; his life as Little Buck brought with it the now muscular toned body of a man, tanned skin fading from summer. Getting under the hide, as thoughts of Sundew filled his mind, he could feel his member was suddenly erect, which hadn't happened to him since he was twelve or thirteen in Iowa City when Becky Byrne was teasing him and showing him her slip. At first, he squirmed with the thought that he had always been told masturbation would eventually turn a man crazy. While he didn't believe it, he didn't want to take a chance and finally fell asleep.

CHAPTER THIRTY-TWO

Back in Topeka, Kansas, Matt had gathered around forty men and their rifles to go to designated points in the town in case the raiders came back. A mail carrier told him the next day that on January 29, 1861, Kansas had been voted as a free state, which had passed in the second session, and soon Topeka became the capital and that because of that, federal troops were engaged with a couple hundred Quantrill raiders on the Missouri border. Matt figured Domingo's forces were likely there causing trouble with them and hoped that for now that meant Topeka would remain quiet.

Matt had to head to Leavenworth, Kansas, now called Fort Leavenworth as the Union Army took it over for a frontier post, to resupply with ammo. Before going there, he thought he might as well ride to Lawrence, which was only about twenty-six miles away.

CHAPTER THIRTY-THREE

In the morning, Kitty was feeding the girls when, through the window, she noticed a rider at the hitching rail. Looking out, it was Matt on Timber. Matt had a beaming smile as he approached Kitty, still in her nightclothes. Quickly giving her a big Texas hug and, knowing he had less than an hour to spare before heading to the fort, he was looking forward to spending whatever time he could with her. He enlightened her as best as he could in that short time regarding all that had transpired, before setting out for the fort. While there, he loaded up with ammo, also buying a Spencer single shot for a cheap price as well as a Sharps .44 rifle.

Back in Topeka, Matt could see nothing much happened while he had been out of town. He had picked up a copy of the Wichita Eagle News at the fort to brush up on the details of all the events across Kansas recently.

CHAPTER THIRTY-FOUR

In April 1861, when rebel troops fired on the federal Fort Sumter in South Carolina, it marked the true beginning of the Civil war. In Topeka, a small garrison of union troops began occupying the capital. Of course, with the vote for statehood, the fighting intensified as William Quantrill's raiders were killing and looting across many small towns.

CHAPTER THIRTY-FIVE

Back with Little Buck, as the warm weather arrived, he went on a spring hunt to replenish the tribe's fresh meat. Coming back to the village, Sundew invited him to her teepee for a tasty meal. After the meal, he did his best to muster up words.

"Where is your grandmother?"

Sundew told him she was visiting her cousin on the far edge of the camp.

Sitting on the bear rug, as close to her as he had ever been, Little Buck did his best to understand what she was saying. Being a typical woman, she told him many things that probably a young teen squaw might talk about. As he could only catch a few words, he was mostly taking in her slender and graceful form, the body of a true Arapaho woman. However, she was a pretty catch for someone, and Little Buck was hoping that he might be that someone. As she went on with her chatting, he made his move, reaching out and clutching her hand. She looked at him and smiled, squeezing his hand. He knew for certain that she must feel the same way. Holding hands, the Irishman and the Indian were locked in a romance. However, he knew he couldn't stay too long, as he didn't know how to act in the case of an Arapaho romance and didn't want to risk doing anything that might offend her. Although she was like a magnet, he still had to be super careful. With all that said and done, he bid her goodbye for now and headed for Marcel's teepee.

Marcel smiled. "So, how goes you thus far, lad?"

"I'm learning more words of the lingo, but I get tongue-tied when I'm with Sundew."

Marcel laughed. "The whole village is talking about you and Sundew."

"They are?" He was surprised.

Marcel continued, "That's a good thing. Many are saying that Sundew has constant eyes for you."

"Yeah," he beamed, "I gathered that."

Marcel pulled out a whittling stick and began applying his knife to it, saying, "What you don't know is that Strong Bow also has bids on her."

"Strong Bow on the edge of camp?"

"That's the one, and I hear that soon we will challenge you over her."

Little Buck was shocked, then voicing, "Let Sundew choose."

Marcel chuckled. "That's not the Indian way. At some point, he will call you out for Sundew's hand."

Little Buck gasped, "What kind of challenge?"

Marcel was stern. "To the death!"

Little Buck suddenly became fearful. "Marcel, I've seen him. He's a big warrior, a lot taller than me. I have to go against a man I don't even know and try to kill him?"

"Yes," Marcel said.

Little Buck really got a sinking feeling. "I can't beat him, can I, Marcel?"

"You can't beat him. He got three kills on a raid a few years ago on a Pawnee camp."

"What kind of weapons?"

"I would think Tomahawks."

"Oh my God!" Little Buck said in despair, realizing that's something Patrick would say, but he was now Little Buck.

Marcel defused the tension. "I'm going to help you train to fight with a Tomahawk. In my younger days in French Canada, I fought with an Onondaga over a woman, and I killed him."

Marcel pulled out a Tomahawk from the teepee. "This is a Comanche one that I found in my travels. I also have a Crow one that I traded for many years ago during my time along that Brazos River in Texas."

"What does Strong Bow have?"

"It doesn't matter because I'll show you how to win, how to slash him to death."

Marcel paused, getting in his face. "Starting now, you must face that this is going to happen, and Strong Bow will be more than eager to kill you because you're a big threat to his plans to marry the squaw Sundew."

"Marry her?! Who told you?" Little Buck was shocked.

"Nobody, but that's the reason he wants to put you out of the way."

Little Buck was now in a place he never expected to find himself, thinking all along that he and Sundew were destined to be together.

"Tonight, I will give you the two Tomahawks; bring them to your teepee and get a feel for them. In the morning, if the braves have no chores for you, go into the woods and make war on a small tree. Get used to the one you like. You must fine tune yourself on the weight of each one. You must move forward with the vision that Sundew will be yours forever."

However, Marcel's words didn't help that sickening feeling that overcame him thinking about a fight to the death with a weapon he had never used that would surely cut him to pieces.

CHAPTER THIRTY-SIX

In Lawrence, Kitty was worrying now that the war was underway. It was August, just four months into the war, but the skirmishes in Kansas were getting more frequent and more federal troops were stationed in Lawrence. All she could think was, despite the heavy armed presence, she longed for the protection of her love, Matt.

In Topeka, more troops were coming in because it was the capital. Matt was also lovesick for his lovely girlfriend. Thinking about her back in Lawrence, Matt knew that it was time to give up being sheriff and return to her. With that in mind, he made Roy the temporary sheriff until the town fathers could run an election or until Roy just appointed himself official sheriff. With all that behind him, he set out for Lawrence.

When he finally made it the twenty-six miles to Lawrence, he knew it was the time of day the Quakers were likely to still have Judy and Barbara. Kitty did a double take when she realized the rap on her door was actually Matt. Both embraced, with Matt promising her he was staying for good and that he was no longer sheriff. Kitty was ecstatic to see him and of course it relieved the tension the volatile frontier had brought down upon her.

"Don't worry none, I got enough money for us and the kids for a while."

Kitty got him a cup of coffee. After a good while, Matt, of course, kept looking at her and then clutched her, affirming for Kitty what was on his mind.

Kitty softly said, "Honey, I've got my period."

Damn, Matt thought. *This cowboy must get on another wave of brain beams and somehow excommunicate himself from the burning lust in his loins, at least for now.*

"Kitty," Matt said, "when will the Quakers bring the girls back?"

"In a couple of hours."

Matt suggested that they get a bite to eat. Soon, they were in El Toro's, sitting at a table while the waitress took their orders. As they were enjoying themselves, six men rode up and entered. Matt could see they were southern rebels, as two of them wore confederate patches.

Matt softly whispered, "Stay calm, honey. I don't think they're looking for trouble."

Kitty nodded. After finishing their meals, they left quickly, not wanting to linger while the rebels were there.

Back at her apartment, the Quakers dropped off the girls. Kitty was a little apprehensive that lately, especially since the war started, more Missouri ruffians were coming to town, who were most assuredly with the rebels.

The next day, Matt went to the gun shop part of the general store and bought an advanced .36 percussion Navy revolver that went along with his double barrel action Colt revolver.

Kitty said, "Be careful, honey. I heard a man in town lost a couple of fingers on the single action rim fire."

"Yes," Matt voiced. "He didn't use it properly."

After lunch, Matt put forth, "Hon, I'm going down to the bar to see if I can find any more news of the war."

"Alright, babe. You know everybody's trigger happy."

"I'm aware, Kitty Cat," he said, giving her a peck.

CHAPTER THIRTY-SEVEN

Back with Little Buck and Sundew, they went to the many pools of water running down the mountain to replenish their bladder bags. Being a particularly hot day, Sundew pointed to a short clump of Quaking Aspen Trees near a pool of water. Telling him she was going to strip off her skirt and dive in, she lowered her finger down, indicating for him to stay behind the trees. Then, Sundew jumped into the mountain water. It was refreshingly cold but wouldn't take long for her to warm up. Little Buck listened to her splashing around and cooling herself from the hot day. After about ten minutes of sitting in limbo behind the Aspen Trees, she called out his name for him to walk over, motioning for him to join her.

Little Buck didn't know what to do. She indicated again for him to lose his breech clout and moccasins, turning her head to give him privacy. She made sure to keep an appropriate distance away from him, Of course, what she didn't know was that, despite the cold mountain water, his penis was extended in full mode. After both swam around and enjoyed the cool waters for a while, she again motioned to him, this time to look the other way while she climbed out on the side. This was a special sort of torture for him, but he managed a brief glance at her backside for a few

109

seconds before she got behind the trees. When he climbed out, unbeknownst to him, Sundew was watching him emerge from the water in all his glory through a small view she had pushed aside in the branches and leaves. Having thoroughly cooled themselves off in a part of the majestic Rocky Mountains, they began to head back to the camp, Little Buck carrying her water for her. Once Sundew and her water were both safely back at her teepee, he departed to join some braves on horseback, patrolling the area for any signs of Pawnee or Crow.

Much later, getting back to camp, he went into the woods to practice with the Tomahawks. After a couple of hours or so, he walked back to his teepee. The thought crossed his mind that the Indians had no feelings of shame or need for modesty when it came to having sex, as he had seen, several times, husband and wife having sex with the teepee flap opened, the woman on the ground on all fours with her backside up as her husband entered her from behind. He recalled when the Spanish settled California; Spanish missionaries would teach the Indians about their way of the white man on top, which was called the missionary way.

CHAPTER THIRTY-EIGHT

At Kitty's apartment, Kitty checked her clock on the wall, wondering why the Quakers hadn't yet brought back her two daughters. When even more time elapsed, she walked out and, mounting Matt's horse, Timber, set out for the other side of town. At that same moment, three or four men came rushing out of a nearby saloon and onto the street. She could tell by the looks of their cartridge belts they were likely Missouri ruffians. One of them suddenly grabbed her reins while another grabbed Kitty herself from the saddle. They were all very clearly drunk.

One said, "Hey, what do we have here?" as the men's hands roamed over her.

Kitty screamed and a four-man displacement of Calvary patrolling the area quickly intervened. Matt, exiting a bar, could hear yelling and screaming and recognized trouble. He was shocked to see Kitty on the ground with the soldiers pointing their guns at several men.

Running over, he picked Kitty up when the squad leader said, "Your wife?"

"No, she's my girlfriend."

One man named Lance yelled out, "We were just having a little fun!"

Before anybody blinked an eye, Matt whacked him, and he went down. The other three under the Army's guns didn't move. Lance got up, spitting out a tooth.

The lieutenant bellowed, "You boys saddle up and get out of Lawrence! If I see you here again, I'll arrest you all!"

"You have no authority!" one said.

"The Army has all the authority under the War Act. It's called Martial Law! Now move out!"

Lance mounted his horse, eying Matt, as he said, "Don't sleep well."

"Ride out, now!" the lieutenant yelled.

One of the soldiers looked at Matt, chuckling, "That was a nice hay maker."

Matt grinned. "He's just lucky I didn't shoot him."

Then both Kitty and Matt thanked the troopers.

Kitty scoffed. "Riffraff and scoundrels everywhere!"

Matt then mounted Timber and pulled Kitty up onto the saddle before they headed for the Quakers.

CHAPTER THIRTY-NINE

Once there, "friend" John of the Quakers told them that the buckboard had a cracked wheel and that's why they hadn't brought the girls back over to Kitty's yet. Matt and Kitty waited for the blacksmith to fix the buckboard.

Meanwhile, the Southerners, Lance and the rest, were holding out about ten miles from town in an old, abandoned shed part of a farm.

Lance said to Eli, "That two-bit cowboy's going to feel my wrath, and you all know I'm going to get that high strung bitch!"

His cousins, Porter and Willard were surprised, with Willard saying, "Forget it. Them Yankee dogs are out patrolling. I dunno…"

In their southern drawl, Lance spat, "I'm going to bed that sweet whatever the fuck her name is!" He sneered. "I'll teach her some of our real Georgia manners."

The men laughed. Porter said, "Get over it, Lance. That Yankee sod-buster ain't no pushover."

Lance continued with increasing venom, "Shut yer trap, Porter! Old Lance is going to put something between her pretty legs that she'll never forget."

"Don't be damn foolish," Porter said. "There's plenty of them whores in Abilene or Dodge."

"Fuck Abilene. I want that sweet smelling sizzler."

The men laughed again, fueling Lance even more.

"The Blue Coats are everywhere, and Lawrence and we don't need a shoot out!" Porter argued.

Lance shot back, "Damn you, morons, you boys are going to grab Miss Goody-Fucking-Two-Shoes for old Lance."

CHAPTER FORTY

Finally, Matt and Kitty got back to her apartment. Because of the delay, the Quakers had fed and bathed Judy and Barbara already, so Kitty quietly put the already exhausted girls to bed in their cribs. Matt could see her clothes pushed back from her breasts and walked over, planting a kiss.

"Why don't you rest up a bit, Honey, while the girls are sleeping?"

Kitty, with a broad smile, said "Rest up or get physical?"

Matt matched her grin. She walked over, sliding her hand down the front of his pants, to Matt's sheer surprise.

"Damn, Kitty Cat, I would say you want to play."

She laughed, "Does it snow in Alaska?" Pointing to his clothes, she continued, "Get off with the duds, Cowboy, while I pretty myself up."

Matt did know exactly what that meant, she was plenty pretty just as she was, but he didn't hesitate to start stripping down. However, when she joined him again wearing a short red slip with embroidery that was unlike anything he had ever seen, Matt was suddenly on an even higher pedestal to love this cowgirl. As she reached out to him, Matt out his hand on her slip.

"Wow, darling, where did you get this?"

"From a trader who was selling tons of stuff from what he said was St. Louis"

After doing their thing, they were just laying in bed when Kitty asked Matt, "How did you get that scar on your side?"

"From a Comanche when I was a Ranger. He would have killed me if I didn't get the gun out in time."

Then, both fell asleep. But, after a while, Matt woke up and looked over to Kitty sleeping, so relaxed. Kitty rolled over, awake, looking right at him.

"What's that I see sticking up in the sheets?"

Matt laughed. "I didn't notice."

Suddenly, she pulled off the sheet. "Didn't notice, huh?"

Then they were skin to skin as Matt confessed, "Your skin is like silk; I just want to feel it all over."

"Okay, Ranger. I don't happen to see any detours."

Matt then caressed her breasts and licked them.

Kitty smiled. "See, Tomcat, there are no guardrails around me."

After more intensive love playing, Matt didn't know what day it was or what month it was or even what planet he was on, as they both rocked in unison.

With Lance and his gang, he had Eli ride back into Lawrence and, knowing there were riders all the time in and out, he knew a single rider wouldn't cause any suspicion. His goal was to find out where Kitty was living.

CHAPTER FORTY-ONE

Back with Little Buck, he went with three other Arapaho to Fort Bent, which had been founded by traders more than eager to trade for furs and many other things of the time period. The braves came away with new goods, including the much-cherished metal cookware, knives, cloth, whiskey, and many other things. Little Buck had traded a fur for a necklace for Sundew. When they arrived back at the camp later in the day, he went directly to Sundew's teepee. She welcomed him in, and he gave her the feathered necklace. To her, it was the ultimate symbol of love and honor. Sitting with her, she offered Little Buck some plums she had picked from a nearby plum tree, still blushing from him giving her the gift.

"Hohow," he replied to her, meaning "Thank you".

He could feel the beaming vibrations channeling between them, so he reached over and kissed her gently. She was pleasantly surprised and kissed him in kind.

A few moments later, Sundew's grandmother returned to the teepee, smiling to see them happy and giggling together. However, they all knew that soon the inevitable combat between him and Strong Bow would have to play out. Of course, Sundew never brought it up, but he was sure she was holding back for fear of a horrible outcome.

Little Buck, formerly Patrick Davis, going against a proven warrior. The mere thought cut into him like a sharp knife, especially now that he was even more lovesick over Sundew than ever. He contemplated whether he would indeed be killed as a result of a crazy tradition, fighting to the death over a young squaw, regardless of whether or not she wanted to marry the warrior.

Little Buck went to his patch of the woods to practice throwing the Comanche tomahawk. Knowing that he had one chance to make a rapid throw to Strong Bow's head, he wanted to be sure he could make it count. If his throw was blocked or he missed entirely, he would be left unarmed and then dead.

CHAPTER FORTY-TWO

In Lawrence, Eli went over into one of the many saloons, tying his mount outside of one called The Digger, a rather small place but the faro games were in full swing. Much to his luck, at the bar he noticed two Missouri ruffians were sat drinking rum and whiskey.

Loud enough for them to hear, Eli said, "Damn, this old town's got Yankees and Blue belly's everywhere."

One of the ruffians commented, "Them Yankees are getting their fat noses in our business. Hell, down East Texas way, we keep them darkies in chains and whip them if they act up." He took a drink before gloating, "General Lee already got a couple of battles under his belt."

Then, to Eli's utter surprise, he saw the high-strung bitch, as his brother calls her, ride by in a buckboard. Quickly, Eli made tracks through the swinging doors to his mount and went after her, seeing a blind spot where the wagon was out of sight. He rode beside her with his pistol out. She was forced to stop. Tying his horse behind, Eli grabbed the reins and headed out of town. Unfortunately for him, two teenagers had stopped behind a building to have a smooch and saw the whole thing.

The girl said, "That woman had a gun in her face!"

"Yeah," the boy said.

"We got to get the sheriff." The girl was stressed out, worried for the woman.

"We can't," the tall boy said, "they will know about us!"

"Never mind that!" the girl said firmly, grabbing his hand. "Come on, Tommy, let's tell the sheriff what we saw!"

Running over to the jail, they quickly told Sheriff Dawson everything that had transpired.

Leaving dust, Dawson and his deputy were on their horses and headed to where the kids last saw the buckboard.

Dawson yelled, "He's taking the road into the hills!"

Before Eli could get too far, they intercepted the wagon and arrested him. Kitty was frantic, explaining what happened as she was on the way to pick up her girls from the Quakers.

Of course, Matt was told, and the whole thing came together that it had been those Georgia men from a few weeks ago.

In the jail, Eli remained closed mouthed. Sheriff Dawson told him that he could possibly hang for trying to waylay the young woman.

Matt had decided he wasn't going to wait around for the sheriff or even an Army detachment; he was going to settle this once and for all.

CHAPTER FORTY-THREE

Back at Kitty's apartment, having picked up the girls, she knew what he was going to do.

"No, Matt, honey, there are still three of them! Don't you dare go after them!"

Matt grabbed her. "Babe, you know what was going to happen to you if those kids didn't sound the alarm. I am not waiting for anybody to settle it!"

She tried to stop him as he mounted Timber, but he was too quick.

Matt knew the area enough to know that there was an abandoned shack around ten or twelve miles away, and he was betting that was where the scumbag was going to take her. So, with his Colts and his Henry rifle, Matt set out, knowing he had to make haste as it would soon be dark, and the gang would be wondering what happened to Eli. Getting behind some brush, he saw a campfire in the distance. As he got closer, he saw Lance stoking the fire while Porter and Willard were doctoring up a deer they had killed.

Willard grumbled, "Where the hell's that Eli?"

"Yeah," Lance was concerned. "That jackass shoulda been done back by now."

Porter laughed, "Knowing him, he's putting them whiskey shots in his belly."

Lance responded, "Yeah, maybe, but I's told him no fucking off. I want to know where that bitch lives!"

So, Lance and the rest had no choice other than to wait for Eli.

Morning unfolded and Matt rolled up his bedroll, glad that no varmints spooked Timber during the night. He could smell coffee, so he made his move and got practically in their backyard.

He yelled, "Drop the guns!!"

However, they dove for cover as the Henry blazed, killing Willard. Lance blasted his revolver toward Matt, mushrooming dirt going flying in front of him, but a bullet winged Lance in the arm.

Matt yelled down again, "Drop the weapons!"

"Okay, okay," Lance bellowed.

Matt slowly walked over, but Porter bolted to a high rock as Lance hoped it would be enough of a distraction and moved for his gun. Lance thought wrong, as a slug hit him in the head, killing him instantly.

Porter knew he was likely dealing with a lawman due to his efficiency with a gun, so he shouted, "I's give up!"

"Throw your weapons out!"

Porter threw both his guns down, hollering, "Don't shoot!"

"I won't shoot," Matt said back, waiting a couple of moments before shooting him in the chest.

The shock on his face was extraordinary as he gasped, "You said you wouldn't shoot!"

"Yeah, I lied. I don't coddle rapists, he said, as Porter died on the spot. Finding an old shovel in the farm shack, Matt buried them.

Returning to Sheriff Dawson, he informed him the men were killed in a gunfight. Of course, the sheriff knew that at one time, Matt himself was the sheriff in Topeka, so he had no cause to question him. Matt knew Eli would spend time in a Texas prison where many prisoners didn't take kindly to attempted rape, especially from someone whose life wasn't worth a red cent.

CHAPTER FORTY-FOUR

Marcel, at the Arapaho village, walked over to Little Buck's teepee, telling him that in the span of three moons, or three days' time, the fight between him and Strong Bow would take place in a 20' x 16' area marked with red dye in the middle of the camp. Of course, in the last three months, he had been following the path in the woods, coaching Little Buck on fighting with a tomahawk and shield. Unfortunately, Little Buck was far from confident in the outcome of the match.

The dreaded day of the battle to the death at last arrived. Both braves were adorned with warpaint. Little Buck grabbed his Comanche tomahawk, which had a long wooden handle and a razor-sharp blade. Strong Bow, also holding a Comanche tomahawk, was an imposing figure in his breech clout and moccasins. He stood nearly 6'3", his body rippled with muscles, and the stare on his face was death-defying and stone cold.

Chief Stone Bear told them of the rules, which Marcel explained more carefully to Little Buck, noting that if anyone gets pushed out of the red line it would be a fatal mistake and the surrounding braves would kill him immediately in a hail of arrows. Little Buck tried not to show fear as Strong Bow kicked off the moccasins for a better feel of the turf. They danced around each other, taking in their opposing defenses. Marcel knew that Strong Bow was by far stronger and had already killed many opponents, but Little Buck was more agile and much swifter. Strong Bow swung his tomahawk at Little Buck, but it was too wide. Little Buck took a swipe, but it was deflected by the other man's shield. Marcel had advised him to keep Strong Bow at bay as long as possible to wear him down, which Little Buck did, as Strong Bow lunged repeatedly trying to make contact with his weapon.

The whole village was focused on their every move and somewhere in the crowd was Sundew. Now, madder and more determined to kill the man he deemed a vile imposter and nothing more than another white man whose goal was to destroy Indians and take their tribal lands, Strong Bow held his weapon high. Little Buck knew he might try to fling it into his head. The contest had already gone on for about forty minutes, and the two men were both drenched in sweat, though they were far from tired. However, Strong Bow, in his raging venom to kill the former soldier, became careless. Little Buck observed this and decided to use deception in combination with Strong Bow's blind rage. He pretended to slip and went down, face first, then in an unprecedented roll of his body just as Strong Bow charged him, Little Buck let loose with his tomahawk, directly into Strong Bow's neck.

CHAPTER FORTY-FIVE

The tribe was shocked that sheer trickery had fooled the greater warrior just had he had rushed over, hand high, to slay Little Buck. Little Buck's timing and accuracy couldn't have been better. He had practiced similar maneuvers many times against Marcel, but none had ever been executed so perfectly.

Blood poured out of Strong Bow's neck, and he died with a gurgling rasp. Complete silence had overtaken the tribe. Some of Strong Bow's blood had sprayed on Little Buck, mixing with the sweat, mud, and warpaint that covered him. The stillness of the tribe was eerie when suddenly, breaking through the crowd, Sundew ran over, embracing him and looking deep into his eyes. Seeing this, the whole tribe knew that Little Buck was her one and only love.

Chief Strong Bow walked over with Marcel, leading the young warrior through the crowd as they all smiled back at him. Then, following a short council with the chief and lesser chiefs, Little Buck and Sundew left the village, holding hands and heading for the cool waters of the mountain stream. Without hesitation, both jumped in. Sundew was rife with happy emotions as they just kissed and hugged.

When they returned to the village, Sundew's grandmother made a great meal, which they enjoyed while relaxing on a deer hide, where Sundew confessed to him that she wanted to become his wife.

CHAPTER FORTY-SIX

Matt rode up to Kitty's apartment and headed inside, where she started on making him some coffee.

Matt said, "Babe, let me have whiskey."

Kitty knew something was up and she stood for a moment, staring into his eyes.

"What is it, Matt?"

He took a long swig of whiskey before he got up and stared out the window.

"Kitty, I think we should leave Lawrence and go to Topeka. Of course, you know Lincoln freed the salves on January first, and this town is right in the cross-hairs of the pro-slavers. It's only going to get worse because all they want is revenge!"

"Yes," she said. "I agree with you."

"Honey," Matt further highlighted, "you dodged a bullet with killers from Georgia, but even though the Army's here I can see more of those rednecks from Missouri coming into town in droves. Plus, there's a rumor the Army is going to cut back here to join with troops in Vicksburg."

"Where would we stay?"

"Don't worry, love, I know everyone in town, no problem."

CHAPTER FORTY-SEVEN

Fast track to August 1, 1863, Matt was now Deputy to Sheriff Roy Jackson. Of course, the Quakers didn't want to leave at first, but their pacifist practices allowed them to see the telltale signs, just as Matt had, that Lawrence was going to be a lot more trouble. On the morning of August 21st, William Quantrill's raid of Lawrence resulted in much of the town being burned and somewhere between 160 and 190 men and boys had been killed, the majority of which had been unarmed. The massacre infuriated the country and Quantrill was in every lawman's gun site. Word reached Topeka of what had happened, and the town went into a lock down, which lasted for some time.

CHAPTER FORTY-EIGHT

Kitty liked her new apartment, which had been recently built and was more than enough room for her children as well as Matt and herself. Barbara and Judy, now eight and nine, were put into a school, much to the irritation of the Quakers, as they were no longer needed and now had two less people to potentially join their belief system.

CHAPTER FORTY-NINE

With the Arapaho, Marcel told Little Buck that Chief Stone Bear was informed that the great Chief Sitting Bull and Crazy Horse were gathering many tribes in the area because of the threat of many Blue Coats coming into their lands.

"What do you think it means?" Little Buck asked.

Marcel shook his head. "It sounds like the embers are burning toward war."

For Little Buck, the greatest concern overtook him, just when things seemed to be smoothly and cementing his assimilation into the tribe and his love for Sundew, now this was unwelcome news. Then, worrying the unthinkable could happen, he realized he could be at war with his own people. Knowing also the U.S. Army had the most manpower and weapons by far, the Indians would be on the short end of the stick. The red men, who, like the Arapahos, could be no more.

Little Buck then decided to join Sundew. Inside her teepee, he told her about his fears with Indians everywhere at war, especially the Arapaho Cheyenne nation, and insisted they should marry soon. She agreed and the chief was told of their decision. The whole tribe was happy for them. However, since the wedding was to be held the following week, they would not have enough time to prepare the full traditional ceremony.

Sundew was clad in a beautiful white, red, and black dyed skirt with necklaces and feathered bracelets around her wrists. Little Buck wore his breech clout, leggings, and moccasins, along with a fancy leather vest that Sundew's grandmother had made for him. With only a little bit of ceremony, at last they were wed. They were given their own teepee and they went inside after the women of the tribe made and gave Sundew some beautiful jewelry made from fish bones and soft rocks, and gave Little Buck a Parfleche, which was a flat carrying case. Inside the teepee there was lots of pretty wildflowers which were later called Colorado blue columbine, fire-weed, and Indian paintbrush.

Little Buck and Sundew looked at each other as a straw bed loomed in the corner. Sundew, then remembering long before her mother died from the fever how she had told her that once married she must immediately submit to her husband by taking all her clothes off and getting on all fours so her husband can have sex. Little Buck of course knew that she would do that, but instead instructed her to lay down on her back. Sundew became confused.

He undressed himself and said, "No, Sundew, I want to love you the way of the white man," as he began kissing her all over.

To Sundew, everything that Little Buck did to her was a paradigm in the making of all the whole sexual experience to the letter. Even after they both climaxed twice, Sundew just couldn't let go of her new husband. Knowing that she was caught up in a deep, unconditional love that matched his own, he just whispered into her ear how much he loved her.

Sundew hid the pain she first felt, but then the second time she had a smile on her face that Little Buck thanked God for. He was sure of making it all possible.

A few days later, Sundew couldn't help telling her best friend of how she had sex and before long almost the whole tribe was told what Sundew had said about "The missionary way".

CHAPTER FIFTY

Matt's covered wagon rolled into Topeka, as he had brought some furniture and odds and ends for their apartment. Then, with the help of the landlord and a few friends, they unloaded it.

"So," Matt gleaned, "what do you think, Kitty Cat? Does this abode have your approval? I know you've lived in Indiana and at one time in a small town south of Boston."

Kitty smiled, "Oh, yes, my ex-Ranger, ex-sheriff, now-deputy, I think it was good planning on your end."

"Okay," he said, "but you really have made the whole apartment homey."

"Thank you, it's called the woman's touch."

Matt then highlighted, "A few days ago, I made a deal with a couple of farmers a few miles out of town to bring milk for the little ones, I also stocked up on whale oil, candles, and kerosene lamps."

Then Matt looked over to the girls. "How do they like the school?"

"They seem to like it a lot. It's less restrictive than the Quakers."

The next day, the landlord, William Ryder, took the whole family to a diner called Bessie's, owned by Horace and Bess Blood, where the food was always very good. After they ate, the men enjoyed whiskey while the women and children drank cider,

Matt put out, "The west is expanding; the railroad is now going through to Nebraska." He hesitated a moment before continuing. "However, this new west is going to cause havoc with the Comanches,"

"I agree," said Ryder. "But everyone in town owns a rifle."

CHAPTER FIFTY-ONE

A few months rolled on; Kitty knew that Matt had a steady job as the deputy sheriff and Topeka was far less dangerous than Lawrence, with only the usual things like rowdy cowboys getting out of hand. Of course, the Quakers weren't happy about not having the girls under their teaching, but as she had told Matt, they could sometimes be overbearing and polarizing. Then, she heard a four-man crew in a rail-wagon checking out railroad ties were ambushed by Comanches. Three were killed and one managed to survive by faking his death, although all of the men had been scalped!

CHAPTER FIFTY-TWO

As summer went into fall, Matt was presently having a drink with his landlord William Ryder when he overheard a cowboy talk of a plan by Colonel John Chivington to attack the Arapaho Cheyenne village at Sand Creek.

Matt went over, introducing himself, "I'm Matt Davis, deputy sheriff. Is this talk for real?"

"Yeah," the man said. "I believe so. That's why I had to get out of Denver. Chivington is looking for volunteers. He's an Indian hater from way back, and I heard he's already got over six hundred volunteers. He calls the Indians prairie worms!"

Later, Matt told Sheriff Jackson what he had overheard.

Jackson put out, "I've heard of Chivington; he's a real Indian hater, so I wouldn't doubt it."

Matt then thought that Sand Creek was just south of the Arapaho village where his brother lived.

CHAPTER FIFTY-THREE

Then, on the early morning of November 29, 1864, a 725-man force of Colorado volunteers attacked the village of Sand Creek, where Arapaho Cheyenne were camped, resulting in a massacre of at least 350 men, women, and children. It was one the worst atrocities perpetrated on native Americans. The women were not only raped but tortured as well, with many having their breasts cut off then were used as tobacco pouches. Children were found cut in half by swords. The rage of the troopers were pushed on by Chivington and in U.S. History was was called the Sand Creek Massacre. Black Kettle, the chief, along with a few others, managed to escape with their lives. Colonel Chivington was called to Washington and reprimanded, especially bragging about it.

Now, Matt knew the spark had been ignited for all the Pains Indians to come together to fight again with the whites in a new Indian war that nobody really wanted. Chief Stone Bear called a council for war to join tribes under Sitting Bull and Crazy Horse to fight the long knives. So, the rest of the year and well into part of 1865, Topeka was on guard for any Indian raids, even through April when Lee surrendered to Ulysses S. Grant, ending the Civil War.

CHAPTER FIFTY-FOUR

However, months later, Northern Carpetbaggers were coming in from the East, buying up farmland for practically pennies and becoming landlords to people who supported the South and were broke and couldn't hold onto their houses, farms, and land. Many pushed back, like the James Gang and the Younger Brothers, who became outlaws to some and saviors to others. William Quantrill was finally shot by Union forces in Kentucky and later died in a hospital.

With all this new chaos, Topeka was now more volatile than ever. At the bars, gun play wasn't uncommon, and the outlying farms were under constant threat. One cool May day, Matt and Kitty wanted to ride their mounts, but Matt knew they shouldn't venture too far because of the new Indian trouble. A couple of mothers that Kitty befriended at the school watched the girls as Matt on Timber and Kitty on Lacey rode to an outcropping of rocks. They dismounted their horses, but hiding in a deep slope were two Comanches. At the same time, also entering the picture, was a fur trapper riding a sorrel; immediately Matt recognized him as Billy Blood, son of Horace and Bess Blood from the restaurant.

Suddenly, a Comanche arrow winged him. Matt drew his gun, telling Kitty to get behind a big rock, which she obeyed, as Matt went after the renegades. Unbeknownst to him, there were four more of them hidden, edging closer to Kitty. Matt drove off the two Comanches and came to the aid of Billy Blood, helping him from his mount. At the same time, the remaining Comanches grabbed Kitty.

"Hold on, kid!" Matt yelled as he jumped on Timber and started after them. One of the Comanches had a rifle and shot at him, knocking him clean off his horse. Blood managed to pull the arrow from his wrist and made his way over to Matt, who had a crease from the rifle, but it knocked him to the ground, immobilizing him for a number of minutes. This, of course, gave the Comanches time to make their escape with a very distraught Kitty.

CHAPTER FIFTY-FIVE

By the time Blood and Matt got back to Topeka and formed a posse, the Indians were long gone. Kitty was forced to ride with a Comanche on his paint as the four band went deeper into Nebraska. Kitty was beside herself, thinking they would likely use her as a bargaining chip to secure rifles or something else, noting they only had two long rifles. One looked like a Burnside Carbine, which she recognized because her cousin Jake had owned one. Kitty was extremely worried what they were going to do with her. Their leader, she gathered, was called Peta, a fierce warrior in full paint with battle scars all over his body. The others seemed to follow his every move.

After riding for quite a distance, they rode into a canyon, which opened up into a river. Peta motioned to dismount, then Kitty was roughly thrown down onto the grass. Peta and the rest had food in a Parfleche pouch and started to eat when Peta told one of the warriors to give her a piece of meat. It looked like it had been dried and had come from some small game. She gagged just looking at it. The warrior motioned for her to eat it, which led her to believe they were indeed going to use her for ransom, perhaps for rifles, or to give her to another tribe as a slave. She knew the reputation of the Comanches, and she dreaded to think that most of the time any captives, regardless of if they were men, women, or children, were tortured.

As they sat chewing the dried meat, the brave closest to her started to tug on her clothes, but Peta yelled something, clearly giving him a tongue lash. Before long, she was back riding double with another brave. As sunset came, they rode into an Indian camp. Kitty was weary from riding so long, her legs ached and the horror of what was happening bubbled up inside of her, knowing that at only 27-years old, her outlook was bleak. She knew that Matt didn't have any idea where she was and couldn't see how he might pull off another miracle and finding her the way he had found his brother.

She soon learned she was in a Kiowa encampment and remembered she had heard of an alliance between the Comanches and the Kiowas. Peta brought her over to the Kiowa chief, Black Jacket. The next thing Kitty knew, Peta and the other Comanches rode off and she was given to three squaws. The women led her and pushed her into one of the large teepees the Kiowas were known for, before they ripped off her clothes, leaving Kitty frozen in fear. They put her in a full Indian dress, and Kitty thought her fate must be slavery.

CHAPTER FIFTY-SIX

She was soon proven correct, as the chief's wife, called Star Dawn, now owned her. Kitty was made to do all the carrying and endless sewing of the braves' and squaws' clothes. The Indian name for slave, to most tribes, was 'Panis', so that is all Kitty was called. At first, the chief's wife would yell at her, a few times using a small stick across her back because Kitty didn't always understand what she wanted her to do. However, after a month or so, the wife slowly began to treat her better.

CHAPTER FIFTY-SEVEN

In Topeka, Matt was, of course, devastated, and was planning to ride to the Arapaho camp to his brother, hoping he might somehow be able to help him. Of course, he knew now that riding to his brother was almost surely a suicide mission after the events of Sand Creek. He decided he would try to put together a well-armed number of volunteers as soon as possible.

CHAPTER FIFTY-EIGHT

As Kitty was experiencing her second month with the Kiowa, she heard children yelling and the Indians were running over to a bearded white man with a pack mule, laden down with trading goods. She wanted so much for him to notice her, but she didn't want to feel the wrath of Star Dawn's stick across her back. One squaw yelled to her to carry some firewood. Evidently, the shrill sound of the squaw caught the white trader's attention, and he looked over.

He walked over, saying, "That face, I know that face from Fort Des Moines."

Kitty's heart rushed to her throat in a flash. She remembered him now too. Zeke now stood in front of her.

"You're the woman who took up with Matt Davis. Sorry, I don't recall your name."

"Kitty," she nearly cried.

Zeke could immediately read the peril that she was in as a slave. He winked at her discretely before making his way back to the Kiowas and continuing to trade. Kitty didn't know what Zeke meant by winking.

A long hour passed when Chief Black Jacket and his wife Star Dawn, along with Zeke, confronted her as she was gathering more wood.

Zeke grinned. "Kitty, I just bought you."

Kitty's mouth fell open, unable to move her tongue to speak.

Zeke further said, "It just about cost my whole stash. I'm going to smoke a pipe with Chief Black Jacket, so it won't be long before we leave."

She was so relieved that her entire body seemed to melt, deflating of all the pent-up gloom. Just then, she remembered she wasn't the only slave. A squaw from another tribe had been here at least five years and, like her, she also had wore a red Kiowa dress, but over the years it had had disintegrated. The squaw slave had escaped and been recaptured, resulting in them whipping her and cutting her tongue out. After that she was only clad in a breech clout and was naked from the waist up.

Kitty had always worn a beautiful Christian cross and managed to hide it from the Comanches when they abducted her. Luckily, again, she somehow hid it from the Kiowas as well. Zeke returned from smoking a peace pipe.

"We'll be pushing on in a couple of hours, after we share a wild turkey with some of the tribe."

Kitty pointed to the squaw slave. "Zeke, I have a cross, inlaid with gold flakes; do you think that you could say it's yours and offer to buy her? She's in an awful way."

Zeke was taken aback. "You want me to buy the squaw with your cross?"

"Yes, she has no hope. She's been whipped and they cut out her tongue."

Zeke could only say, "You're a good Christian woman, ma'am. Give it to me, I'll see what I can do."

When Star Dawn saw it glitter in the sun, she wanted it without question. Kitty approached the squaw and, in using what little bit of Indian language she had picked up, miming the rest, she explained that the woman was free and could leave with them and it was the only time she saw her smile. Finally, Zeke, Kitty, and the squaw rode out of the Kiowa camp.

CHAPTER FIFTY-NINE

Many miles out, they stopped for water. Kitty walked over to Zeke, hugging him for saving her and the squaw.

"How can I ever repay you?"

"No, ma'am, no need to. Matt and I go way back."

Kitty handed a flask of water to the squaw, who was now wearing one of Zeke's shirts.

Zeke said, "We're in Southern Wyoming. In about three days, we should reach Topeka, as long as we don't run into any snags."

They continued on for two days; on the third morning, Zeke was making some coffee and told Kitty to awaken the squaw, unsure if she would like some as well.

Kitty went over to where she lay. She stopped in her tracks and called for Zeke as she began to cry. Zeke could see the squaw had died.

Kitty held her face in her hands. "Why, Zeke? What happened?"

"I don't know, it really could be anything."

Kitty, still crying, said, "I was going to help her when we got back, help her to live her life again."

Zeke offered, "You helped her to die a free woman."

Zeke took a small shovel from his saddlebag, and they buried her.

Kitty sobbed, "I never even knew her name or her tribe, but I'm sure she'll be in God's arms."

"Yes," Zeke voiced. "Always remember that because of you, she at least died free."

CHAPTER SIXTY

In Topeka, Matt was in the process of putting together a twenty-five-man posse to search for Kitty when he saw two riders coming into town, leaving him in complete and utter shock. He couldn't believe his eyes; it was his old friend Zeke riding in with Kitty. The look on Matt's face was priceless. He rushed to her in complete disbelief. Having then reunited, seeing her in an Indian dress, he knew it was unbelievable that Zeke happened to go to the Kiowas to trade and managed to save her in the process.

The next day, they both stirred as the Sun came up. Matt looked deep into Kitty's eyes.

"Gal," he said, "I just got a terrific idea."

"Oh, yeah? What's that, cowboy?"

"Let's get married."

Kitty was enthralled, saying, "Are you serious?"

He laughed, "Does Kentucky moonshine have a kick to it?"

Kitty quietly asked, "When, Mr. Matt?"

"Soon, because Zeke won't stay too long, and I want him to be my best man."

"Okay then, how soon?"

"Oh, soon."

"Yes, I know that, but how soon?"

"Oh, soon, soon, soon."

"Quit playing, Matthew! How soon, soon, soon?"

"Darling, it's soon, soon, and more soon."

Kitty grabbed him. "I'll soon you then!"

She twisted his arm up, "Now, boyfriend, do I have to force it out of you?"

"Okay, okay, I give up as soon as I put my lips to yours."

When they finally got up and had breakfast with the girls, Kitty told them she and Matt would be getting married next week. Judy and Barbara were excited.

CHAPTER SIXTY-ONE

So, in the afternoon of May 4, 1869, they were married at the Methodist church.

After all the hoopla, that night Matt said, "Well, Kitty Cat, now that we're married, shall we, as they say, consummate it?"

"You're a riot, Matt Davis."

"What do you mean, Mrs. Davis?"

They both laughed then went into the bedroom as the Moon shone over the Kansas Sky.

Printed in the United States
by Baker & Taylor Publisher Services

Printed in the United States
by Baker & Taylor Publisher Services